Rain

by
Robert Kalan

illustrated by
Donald Crews

A MULBERRY PAPERBACK BOOK
New York

20 19 18 17

Library of Congress
Cataloging in Publication Data
Kalan, Robert.   Rain.
Summary: Brief text and illustrations
describe a rain storm.
1.   Rain and rainfall—Juvenile literature.
[1.   Rain and rainfall]   I. Crews, Donald.
II.   Title.   QC924.7.K34   551.5'781
77-25312   ISBN 0-688-10479-7

With love to my parents
R.K.

. . . and to mine
D.C.

Blue sky

Yellow sun

White clouds

Gray clouds

No sun

RainRain
RainRainRain
inRainRainRain
nRainRainRainRain
RainRainRainRain
RainRainRainRain
RainRainRainRain

Gray sky

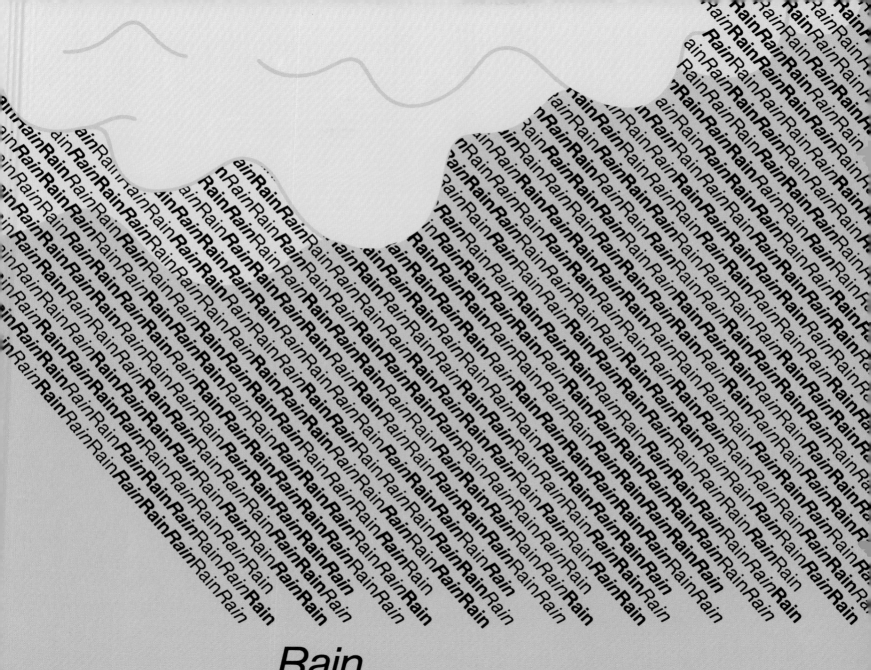

Rain

Rain on the green grass

Rain on the black road

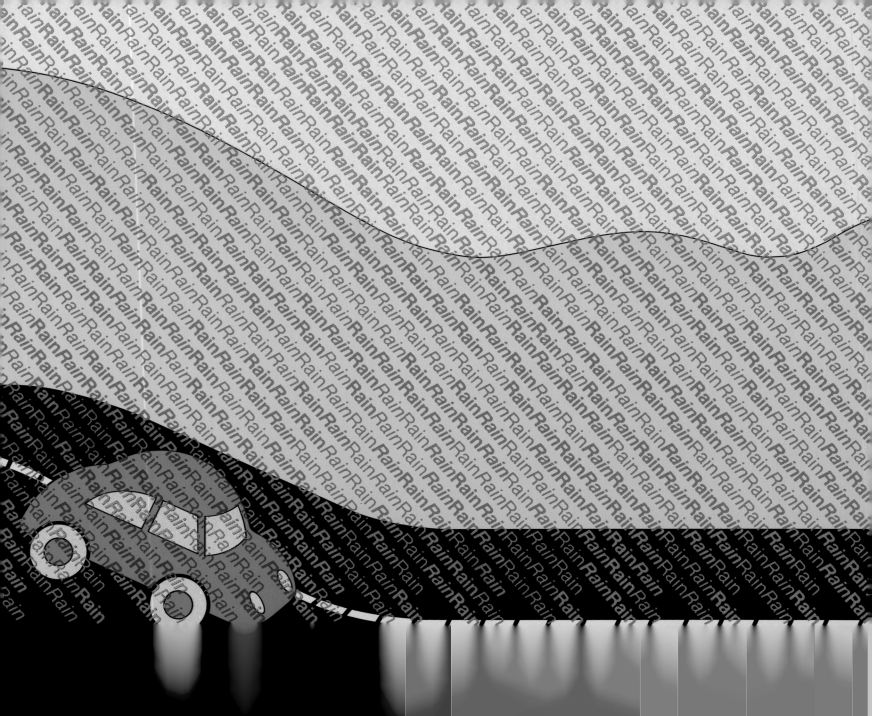

Rain on the brown fence

Rain on the green trees

Rain

Rain

RAINBOW

ROBERT KALAN was born in Los Angeles. He was graduated from Claremont Men's College.
He has taught reading to both gifted and remedial students as well as kindergarten and fourth grade, and completed a master's degree in education at Claremont Graduate School. He is currently living in Bellevue, Washington.

DONALD CREWS was graduated from Cooper Union for the Advancement of Science and Art in New York City. He has written and illustrated many books for young children, including We Read: A to Z and Ten Black Dots. He and his wife, Ann Jonas, are freelance artists and designers, and live in New York.